SPOOKY
and the Witch's Goat

By Natalie Savage Carlson · Illustrated by Andrew Glass

Lothrop, Lee & Shepard Books   New York

*To Geri-Marie Bushey,
the little sister of Michelle and Laura,
"the miracle twins"*

N. S. C.

For Mary Price and her students

A. G.

*Library of Congress Cataloging in Publication Data
Carlson, Natalie Savage. Spooky and the witch's goat.
Summary: Two cats protect their catnip bed from the "witch's goat" at great cost to the goat.
[1. Cats—Fiction] I. Glass, Andrew, Ill. II. Title. PZ7.C2167Sov 1989 [E] 88-21628
ISBN 0-688-08540-7 ISBN 0-688-08541-5 (lib. bdg.)*

The Bascombs had a big black cat with green eyes named Spooky. And they had a little white cat named Snowball. Spooky and Snowball had once belonged to the witch who lived in the woods down the road.

At night Spooky and Snowball liked to go out in the
back yard and roll in their catnip bed. Then they would
climb up on the fence and watch the stars come out,
twinkle, twinkle.

One night when they were watching the stars, a great, shaggy goat with one horn in the middle of his head jumped over the fence. The goat went to the petunia bed and ate some petunias. Munch, crunch, gulp! Munch, crunch, gulp!

Spooky and Snowball watched the goat eating the flowers. They didn't care.

Next night they rolled in the catnip bed as usual, then climbed up on the fence. They watched the one-horned goat jump into the yard again. He went to the begonia bed and ate some begonias. Munch, crunch, gulp!

Spooky and Snowball watched him eat the flowers. They didn't care.

But the Bascombs cared.

In the morning the Bascomb mother said to the Bascomb father, "Some bugs are getting our flowers. You better spray them well."

So the Bascomb father did.

That night the one-horned goat came over the fence again. He began eating some peonies. Munch, crunch, spit-tooey! He spat them out. The sprayed flowers tasted worse than skunk cabbage.

So he went to the catnip bed. He began eating the catnip. Munch, crunch, gulp!

Now Spooky and Snowball cared. It was their catnip.

Spooky crept slinky, sly along the fence until he reached the catnip bed. He spat, *Pfft, pfft.* The goat just looked at him out of one eye and went on eating.

Spooky wanted that goat out of the catnip bed *now*.
He jumped on the goat's back and dug his claws into its
shaggy hair.

Ma-a-a! The goat jumped straight up in the air. He
bucked and kicked, but Spooky held on.

The goat jumped over the fence, but still Spooky held on.

The goat raced down the road, tlot, tlot, tlot. Spooky held on.

The goat raced past the haunted house, tlot, tlot, tlot. Spooky held on.

The goat raced to the woods, tlot, tlot, tlot. Spooky held on until they neared the witch's hut under the witch hazel tree. Aha, the goat belonged to the wicked witch!

Spooky jumped down and ran home high-tail and lickety-split.

He and Snowball rolled in the catnip bed.

The very next night the goat was back. He went to
the catnip bed again. Munch, crunch, gulp!

Spooky was furious. He jumped down from the fence and crawled over to the goat. His hair stood on end. His claws were bared. He howled and yowled and spat. *E-YOW! E-YOW! PFFT! PFFT!*

The goat whirled around. *MA-A-A!* He lowered his horn to butt Spooky.

But Snowball jumped down from the fence and grabbed the goat's short tail in her claws. He bucked and kicked to shake her loose.

Then Spooky grabbed the goat's long beard. The goat rose up on his hind legs to shake Spooky loose. Up, Spooky! Down, Snowball! Up and down, seesaw, seesaw! But the cats hung on.

The goat raced out of the yard, tlot, tlot, tlot. He started down the road, bouncing the cats along.

Such a sight had never been seen on that road.

The stars blinked with surprise. One of them fell out of the sky.

The moon hid behind a cloud.

With a cat here and a cat there, the goat raced
through the woods.
    At the witch's hut, he whirled around in one last try
to be free of the cats. Whirligig, whirligig!

Spooky let go of the beard and backed against the
door. *E-YOW! E-YOW! PFFT! PFFT!*

The goat headed for him with lowered horn. But at the last second, Spooky ducked.

CRASH! The goat butted the door so hard his head went through. When he tried to pull it out, he pulled the door off its hinges.

Snowball let go of the goat's tail. The cats hid behind a bush as the angry witch came out of the hut.

"Rogue of rack and ruin!" she shrieked. "I'll fix you good! You'll never cause calamity again!"

She waved her hands over the goat like giant talons
and chanted:

"Goat you are now.
Goat you shall always be.
Shine in the southern sky
For all eternity."

There was a blinding flash and the goat disappeared.
The witch went into her hut to look up the spell for
mending a broken door.

Spooky and Snowball went scoot and skedaddle out of the woods. As they bounded down the road, a new star in the constellation Capricorn—the Goat—blazed above them.

They went through the little door in the big door. They jumped up on the fat chair with the bump in the seat and purred themselves to sleep. Purr, purr.

Next morning the Bascomb girl's eyes were round as the buttons on her blouse.

She said to her family, "You'll never believe what I saw last night."

The Bascomb boy said, "Probably not."

The girl said, "I heard Spooky outside howling and yowling. When I looked out the window, I saw a *unicorn* bouncing the cats up and down."

The Bascomb mother said, "You had a nightmare. That's what happens when you eat pizza at bedtime."

Spooky and Snowball winked at each other. They knew their catnip was safe.